To ....

For being good.

MERRY CHRISTMAS!

From Santa

Santa is coming to Santa Cruz

Written by Steve Smallman
Illustrated by Robert Dunn
Designed by Sarah Allen

Published by Sourcebooks Jabberwocky, an imprint of Sourcebooks, Inc.
P.O. Box 4410, Naperville, Illinois 60567-4410
(630) 961-3900
Fax: (630) 961-2168
www.jabberwockykids.com

Library of Congress Cataloging-in-Publication data is on file with the publisher.

Source of Production: Worzalla, Stevens Point, WI, USA
Date of Production: September 2013
Run Number: 21290
Printed and bound in USA.
WOZ 10 9 8 7 6 5 4 3 2

Santa is coming to Santa Cruz

Written by Steve Smallman
Illustrated by Robert Dunn

sourcebooks
jabberwocky

"Well?"

boomed Santa. "Have all the children from **Santa Cruz** been good this year?"

"Well...uh...mostly," answered the little old elf, as he bustled across the busy workshop to Santa's desk.

Santa peered down at the elf from behind the tall, teetering piles of letters that the children of Santa Cruz had sent him.

"Mostly?" asked Santa, looking over the top of his glasses.

"Yes...but they've all been **especially** good in the last few days!" said the elf.

"Jolly good!" chuckled Santa,
"Then we'd better get their presents loaded up!"

Even though the sack of presents was

really, really big

really, really

and the elves were — small,

they seemed to have no trouble loading it onto Santa's sleigh.
Though how they managed to fit such a big sack into one little sleigh
even they didn't know. But somehow they did.

"Splendid!" boomed Santa. "We're ready to go!"

"Er...not quite, Santa," said the little old elf. "One of our reindeer is missing!"

"Missing?

Which reindeer is missing?" asked Santa.

"The youngest one, Santa," said the elf. "It's his first flight tonight. I've called him and called him, but..."

Just then, a young reindeer strolled up, munching on a large carrot.

"where have you been?"

asked Santa.

But the youngest reindeer was crunching so loudly that it was no wonder he hadn't heard the little old elf calling.

"Oh well, never mind," said Santa, giving the reindeer a little wink. He took out his Santa-nav and tapped in the coordinates for Santa Cruz, California. **"This will guide us to Santa Cruz in no time."**

Crunch!
Crunch!
Crunch!

With a flick of the reins and a jerk of the harness, off they went, racing through the sky.

"Ho, ho, ho!"
laughed Santa.

"We'll soon have all these presents delivered to Surf City!"

Santa's sleigh flew through the starry night, heading south across the Arctic Ocean. On they flew in the wintry air, high above Alaska. In the wink of an eye, the sleigh was flying over the Rocky Mountains and San Francisco.

The youngest reindeer was very excited. He had never been away from the North Pole before.

They had just crossed Mount Bielawski
when, suddenly, they ran into a thick fog.
Mist whirled around the sleigh.

They couldn't see a thing!

The youngest reindeer was getting a bit worried,
but Santa didn't seem concerned.

"In two miles..."

said the Santa-nav in a bossy lady's voice,

"...keep left at the next star."

"But, ma'am," Santa blustered, "I can't see any stars in all this fog!"

Soon they were

hopelessly lost!

Ding-dong!
Ding-dong!

Then, through the
foggy blanket, the
youngest reindeer heard
a faint, ringing sound.

Ding-dong!

He looked over at the old reindeer
with the red nose. But he had
his head down.

(Red nose...I wonder
who that could be?)

Ding-dong!
Ding-dong!

Ding-dong!
Ding-dong!

There was that sound
again, like bells ringing.
The youngest reindeer turned
around to look at Santa.
But Santa wasn't listening.
He seemed to be arguing
with a little box with
buttons on it.

With a flick of the
harness and a jerk of the
reins, the youngest reindeer gave a
sharp *tug* and headed off toward
the sound of the bells, pulling Santa
and his sleigh behind him!

"Whoa!"

cried Santa, pulling his hat straight. "What's going on?" Then, to his surprise, he heard the ringing sound.

"Well done, young reindeer!" he shouted cheerfully, "It must be the bells of the Town Clock Tower. Don't worry, children, Santa is coming!"

Then, suddenly...

CRUNCH!

The sleigh hit something as it plummeted through the fog. **"You have arrived!"** said the Santa-nav unhelpfully.

Finally, when the fog had cleared
and the clouds parted, Santa discovered
exactly where they were...

...stuck, right at the very top of a
Christmas tree near the
City Council building!

"Everybody,
PULL!"

The reindeer *pulled* with all their might until, at last, with a screeching noise, the sleigh scraped clear of the Christmas tree. Santa steered them safely above the Downtown Public Library, over Santa Cruz Mission, past Wagner Grove, and down into Harvey West Park.

Luckily, there was no
real damage done, but
the packages had all been
jumbled up. Santa quickly sorted
the presents into order again.

"All right," said Santa. "Thanks to this
young reindeer I know where we are
now. Don't worry, children,

Santa is coming!"

Santa drove his sleigh expertly from rooftop to rooftop all over Santa Cruz, popping in and out of chimneys as fast as he could go. *pretty fast for a chubby fellow!)*

There were big chimneys in Aptos and small chimneys in Live Oak. He squeezed down thin chimneys in Capitola and plummeted down fat chimneys in San Lorenzo Valley.

The youngest reindeer was
amazed at how quickly they went.
Santa never seemed to get tired at all!
And it looked like all the children in
Santa Cruz were going to be very
lucky this year! But the youngest
reindeer was starting to feel
a bit weary and quite
hungry too!

He piled them under the Christmas trees and carefully filled up the stockings with surprises.

In house after house, Santa delved inside his sack for packages of every shape and size.

Santa took a little bite out of each cookie, a tiny sip of milk, wiped his beard, and popped the carrots into his sack.

In house after house, the good children of Santa Cruz had left out a plate of cookies, a small glass of milk, and a big, crunchy carrot.

From Scotts Valley to Seabright, from Soquel to Bonny Doon, from Felton to Twin Lakes, and ALL the places in between, Santa and his sleigh visited every house in Santa Cruz.

Santa delivered presents to Angel, Abigail,
Benjamin, Brianna, Camila, Christopher...
the list went on and on! ...Yazmine,
Zachary, Zander, Zybil.

(Zybil? That must be a spelling mistake, surely!)

SUPERMARKET

Finally, Santa had delivered the last present on his long Santa Cruz list.

"Great moons and stars!" sighed Santa. "It's past midnight and my sack seems as heavy as ever! I hope I haven't forgotten anyone."

Santa opened his sack to check...but it was full of juicy, crunchy carrots!

Santa divided the carrots among all the reindeer.
"Well, done!" he said, patting the youngest reindeer gently on the nose.

But the youngest reindeer didn't hear him...
he was too busy munching!

Then it was time to set off for home. Santa reset his Santa-nav once more
to the North Pole, and soon they were speeding above Santa Cruz Beach
Boardwalk and out over Monterey Bay through the crisp, starry night.